The Mystery of Spring Gully

Story by Jill McDougall
Illustrations by Olivia Duches

Contents

Chapter 1

A Place of Mystery

Dad had promised to take Violet and Jasper on an adventure in the holidays.

After a long drive, Dad stopped the car in a dusty old town. "Welcome to Spring Gully," said Dad. "It's a place of mystery!"

"How exciting!" said Violet. "I love mysteries!"

"I can see a mystery already," Jasper said.
"There are lots of old buildings, but no people."

"That's right," said Dad.
"No one lives in Spring Gully any more."

"Why did they leave?" asked Violet in amazement.

But Dad only smiled.
"Let's go for a wander," he said.
"You might find some clues."

Violet, Jasper and Dad walked along the street.

"This looks like an important building," said Violet, stopping beside a large doorway.
She read the sign above the door:

"Here's our first clue!" said Violet.
"1903 must be the year everyone left!"

"You're right," said Dad, smiling.
"Now, let's keep walking."

Chapter 2

Paddy McGee

Soon, Violet, Jasper and Dad came to a statue.
The statue was of a man on one knee.
He was holding a pan.

"That man is looking for gold!" said Violet.
"We learned about gold mining at school."

Violet climbed some steps to the statue.
A sign said:

PADDY McGEE
GOLD DIGGER

"Spring Gully must be an old gold town!" said Violet.

"Yes!" replied Jasper.
"Maybe there was no gold to be found after 1903
and that's why everyone left."

Violet turned to Dad.
"Have we solved the mystery, Dad?" she asked.

Dad smiled and nodded.
"But this town has an even bigger mystery," he said.

"What is it?" asked Violet, excitedly.

Paddy McGee
PADDY McGEE
GOLD DIGGER

"You'll find out after lunch," said Dad.

He led the way up several steps to a park.
"We can eat our sandwiches here," he said.

They sat beneath a giant tree.
"This tree is so tall and strong," Violet said.
"I bet it's as old as Spring Gully!"

Chapter 3

At the Museum

After lunch, Dad took Violet and Jasper to a small museum on the edge of town.

"You'll find out about the next mystery here," Dad said.

"I'm Bridie," said the woman in the museum.
"My great-grandfather was Paddy McGee.
You might have seen his statue."

"Yes," said Violet. "Did he find lots of gold?"

Bridie smiled proudly.
"Paddy found a gold nugget as big as a tennis ball!" she said.

"He must have been rich," said Jasper.

"That's the mystery," replied Bridie.
"He hid the gold and it's never been found!"

Chapter 4

Paddy's Treasure

Bridie showed Violet and Jasper an old piece of paper.
"Paddy McGee left us a clue," she said.
"Here, read this note."

To find my greatest treasure ...

Step and step and step, you go.
To reach the top, you will start low.
You'll see me standing tall and strong.
Look inside – you can't go wrong!

Violet and Jasper read the note carefully.
"The treasure is hidden
at the top of some steps," Violet said.

Jasper looked excited.
"The *statue* is at the top of some steps!" he cried.
"Maybe Paddy put the gold nugget inside his statue!"

Bridie smiled sadly.

"The statue was taken apart once," she said.
"There was no gold inside."

"Oh," said Jasper.
"I guess someone found it long ago."

Chapter 5

Solving the Mystery

Everyone was silent for a minute.
Then, Violet said,
"I don't believe Paddy put his gold inside the statue.
The statue shows Paddy McGee kneeling on the ground.
He isn't standing tall and strong like it says in the note!"

"That's right!" cried Jasper.

He suddenly remembered the park where they'd had lunch.

"There are some other steps in town!" he said.

"And they lead to a tall, strong tree!" cried Violet.

A short time later, they arrived at the giant tree. Bridie came with them.

"There's a hollow in this tree," Violet said, excitedly. "I can reach inside!"

Violet pulled out an old bag from under some leaves. The bag felt heavy! Was Paddy's gold inside?

No! Inside was a rock and something else . . . a photo.

"That's a photo of my grandmother
when she was a little girl!" cried Bridie.

On the back, Paddy had written:
Rosie – my greatest treasure.

Dad said quietly, "Paddy's treasure was not gold.
It was his daughter – Bridie's grandmother."

"Thank you, Violet and Jasper," said Bridie.
"You've solved the mystery of Paddy's treasure!"

Violet smiled to herself.
She knew there was one more mystery to solve
in Spring Gully:
Where *did* Paddy hide the gold?